牛
Ox

虎
Tiger

兔
Rabbit

鼠
Rat

龍
Dragon

豬
Pig

For nearly 5,000 years, the Chinese culture has organized time in cycles of twelve years. This Eastern calendar is based upon the movement of the moon (as compared to the Western which follows the sun), and is symbolized by the zodiac circle. An animal that has unique qualities represents each year. Therefore, if you are born in a particular year, then you share the personality of that animal. Now people worldwide celebrate this two-week-long festival in the early spring and enjoy the start of another Chinese New Year.

蛇
Snake

狗
Dog

馬
Horse

雞
Rooster

羊
Sheep

猴
Monkey

To Uncle Hank whose smile, pawshake, and wit established many a friendship. –O.C.

To Alexandra, the utmost authority on all things cute. Without your support and incredible patience, this would not have been possible. I love you. And to my parents whose love, encouragement, and life-long sacrifices have allowed me to follow my dreams. Thank you so very much. You are the best! – J.R.

immedium

Immedium, Inc.   P.O. Box 31846   San Francisco, CA 94131
www.immedium.com

Text Copyright ©2022 Oliver Chin
Illustrations Copyright ©2022 Justin Roth

First hardcover edition (ISBN 978-1-59702-020-6) published 2010.

Edited by Don Menn
Book design by Elaine Chu and Dorothy Mak
Chinese translation by Hsiaoying Chen, Grace Mak, and Dorothy Mak
Calligraphy by Lucy Chu

Printed in China
10 9 8 7 6 5 4 3 2 1

Library of Congress Cataloging-in-Publication Data

Names: Chin, Oliver Clyde, 1969- author. | Roth, Justin, illustrator. |
   Chin, Oliver Clyde, 1969- Year of the tiger. | Chin, Oliver Clyde, 1969- Year of the tiger. Chinese.
Title: The year of the tiger : tales from the Chinese zodiac / written by Oliver Chin ; illustrated by Justin Roth.
Description: San Francisco, CA : Immedium, Inc., 2021 | Originally published in a different form in 2010. |
   Audience: Grades 2-3. | In English and simplified Chinese. | Summary: The adventures and misadventures
   of Teddy the tiger cub as he learns that "good manners make good neighbors." Lists the birth years and
   characteristics of individuals born in the Chinese Year of the Tiger.
Identifiers: LCCN 2021021716 (print) | LCCN 2021021717 (ebook) | ISBN 9781597021562 (hardcover) |
   ISBN 9781597021579 (ebook)
Subjects: | CYAC: Tiger--Fiction. | Animals--Infancy--Fiction. | Astrology, Chinese--Fiction. |
   Chinese language materials--Bilingual.
Classification: LCC PZ710.831 .C6158 2021 (print) | LCC PZ710.831 (ebook) | DDC [E]--dc23
LC record available at https://lccn.loc.gov/2021021716
LC ebook record available at https://lccn.loc.gov/2021021717

ISBN 978-1-59702-156-2

The Year of the Tiger
·Tales from the Chinese Zodiac·
十二生肖故事系列 虎年的故事

Written by Oliver Chin
Illustrated by Justin Roth

文：陈曜豪
图：贾斯汀罗斯

immedium
Immedium, Inc.
San Francisco. CA

In the mighty jungle, the tigers slept each night.
But tonight excitement filled the air. A small cry rang
out. Then catcalls joined it in a great celebration.

The King and Queen just had a baby!

住在诺大丛林里的老虎们，每天晚上都安安稳稳地睡觉，
但是今天晚上空气中弥漫着兴奋的气息。丛林里传出了微微的哭声，
大伙儿们跟着发出吼叫声，开心地加入庆祝。

虎王和虎后的宝宝刚出生了！

As the morning sunshine warmed the royal den, the cub yawned loudly, **"Roar!"**

The Queen whispered, "Hush, my darling."

Cuddling his newborn, the King chuckled, "Theodore, you are a feisty chap."

当早晨的阳光温暖
皇家巢穴时，
小老虎打了一个大大
的哈欠：“吼！”

虎后轻声地说：
“亲爱的，安静下来。”

虎王拥着他刚
出生的孩子，
咯咯地笑：“泰迪，
你这个小家伙
真是活泼。”

Soon this fur ball roamed the forest like it was his own backyard. His parents marveled at his curiosity. Teddy meowed, **"I'm becoming a big cat!"**

The Queen laughed, "Someday you'll be king of the jungle."

很快地，小毛球漫游在丛林里，
就像是他家的后院一样。
他的父母对小老虎的好奇心感到惊讶。
泰迪喵喵叫："我快要变成一只大老虎了！"

虎后笑着说："有一天，你会成为丛林之王的。"

Later she advised, "Son, a wise ruler starts out as a careful prince."

The King added, "We've heard of dangerous animals called 'humans.' Their houses and roads invade our land, so stay away from them."

后来，她提醒小老虎："儿子啊，若要当一位有智慧的治者，你要从一位谨慎小心的王子开始。"

虎王补充说："我们听说有种危险的动物叫做人类。他们侵占我们的土地来盖房子、造道路，记得要离他们远一点。"

But this warning tickled the kitten's interest. **"I want to see these beasts for myself,"** gushed Teddy. He learned that people lived on the edge of the forest. So one evening, he set out alone in that direction.

但是这样的警告却激起了小老虎的好奇心。"我想要亲自去看这些野兽，"他得知人类居住在丛林的边缘，于是一天晚上，他独自往那个方向走去。

After a while he came to a ridge. In the glen below were thatched roofs,
dirt paths, and a person sitting in a field! To get a better look,
Teddy sneaked down the hill and his striped coat blended into the tall reeds.

经过了一段时间，他走到了一座山脊。在山脊下的谷地，有茅草盖的屋顶和泥巴小径，
还有一个人坐在田里！为了要看得更清楚，泰迪蹑手蹑脚地走到了山下，
他身上的条纹恰巧和挡住他的芦苇相仿，让他能躲藏起来。s

The clearing of short grass felt strange under his feet.
Distracted by a rat, he gleefully pounced after it
and snarled, **"Roar!"**

他觉得脚下那一片短草地有种奇怪的触感。
一只老鼠转移了他的注意力，他开心地追逐着老鼠，
然后发出一声吼叫："吼！"

However, he startled the
nearby ox and horse, which
frantically galloped off.

他却惊吓到附近的牛和马，
他们吓得像发狂似地逃跑。

In the moonlight, the girl saw Teddy and froze in surprise.
Su screamed, "Tiger! Tiger!"

The cat scampered into the trees.
Racing back to the palace,
he thought, **"That creature
was quite a fright."**

月光下，小女孩看见了泰迪，
她惊讶地站在原地，一动也不动。
苏惊声尖叫："老虎！老虎！"

小老虎惊慌地跑进了树林。
他用最快的速度跑回皇宫，
他心想："人类真是种可怕的动物。"

Meanwhile, the villagers searched for the intruder. But they found neither hide nor hair of Teddy.

"Su, don't cry 'tiger,' when there isn't one!" chided her father, Ba-Ba.

同时间，村民们正四处搜寻着入侵者的踪影，
但是他们遍循不着泰迪，连他的一根毛发都没找到。

"苏，不要在没看见老虎的时候乱喊老虎！"
苏的爸爸生气地责备她。

At home, Teddy didn't tell his parents about his close encounter. But he couldn't stop thinking about the girl.

So early one morning, he returned to town and spotted the barn where Su fed the livestock.

回到家以后，泰迪并没有将他的遭遇告诉他的父母，但是他一直在想着那个女孩。

于是在一天的早上，他回到了村庄，在村庄里发现了苏喂牲畜的谷仓。

Inside, Su served breakfast to the sheep and pig.
Not wanting to scare anyone, Teddy said,
"Good morning."

Sharp teeth filled the tiger's smile.
The animals squealed,
"Run for your lives!"

苏正在里头喂羊和猪吃早餐。
泰迪并不想要惊动任何人，
他轻声地说："早安。"

泰迪微笑的时候露出他尖尖的牙齿。
动物们尖声大叫：
"快跑！想要活命就快跑！"

Teddy sprang backwards
into a haystack.

Su laughed since she, too, had thought of the tiger. "You must be thirsty,"
she said and poured a bowl of milk. "Here kitty, kitty."

Intrigued, Teddy took a sip. Licking the bowl clean,
the tiger purred, **"I'm Teddy."**

泰迪往后面一跳，跳进了一堆干草里。
苏却跟着泰迪笑了，因为她也想着
小老虎呢。"你一定渴了吧，"

她一边说一边把牛奶倒进碗里。
"快来喝，小猫。"

泰迪好奇地试了一口，
然后把整碗的牛奶喝完，
把碗舔了干净，轻声地说："我叫泰迪。"

Rubbing her nose to his, she replied, "I'm Su. Do you want to play?"

Suddenly, Su's mother opened the door. Teddy jumped outside to the woods beyond.

Staring at the orange blur across her field, Ma-Ma cried, "It's the tiger!"

苏用鼻子磨了磨小老虎的鼻子，然后回答：
"我叫苏。你要不要和我一起玩？"

这时候，苏的母亲突然打开了门。泰迪往外一跃，
跳进远处的树林。

妈妈看着一团橘色的毛发从眼前跑过，
穿越田地，她大声呼叫："这就是那只老虎！"

Ba-Ba told Su to stay inside with the dog,
"Remember, it's better to be safe than sorry!"
Then he and Ma-Ma left to warn their neighbors.

爸爸让苏和小狗待在屋里，说：
"记着，还是小心谨慎一点比较好！"
然后他和妈妈就出门去警告
邻居们这个消息。s

Back in the jungle, the King scowled, "Teddy, we know where you've been. We told you to avoid those people."

The Queen sighed, "The outsiders have gotten too close. Now we must find a new home."

回到了丛林以后，虎王对小老虎沉下了脸，说："泰迪，我们知道你去过哪里了。我是告诉过你要避开那些人类的。"

虎后叹了一口气，"人类离我们太近了。现在，我们必须寻找一个新的家。"

Obediently packing his belongings, Teddy wondered, **"Why are we afraid of them when they are scared of me?"**

But he still wanted to see Su one last time, so he slipped away to the girl's house.

泰迪聪从父母的指令，乖乖地收拾行李，但他忍不住想："我们为什么要怕人类呢？明明人类很怕我的呀！"

但是，他还是很想要再见苏最后一面，于是他又悄悄地溜到小女孩的家。

As the tiger crept closer,
the watchdog growled, "Who goes there?"

Trying to be friendly, Teddy offered
a pawshake, **"Hello, there."**

Yet sharp claws popped out,
and the terrified pooch scampered off.

当小老虎缓慢地靠近的时候，
看门的小狗大声地吠："是谁在那里？"

泰迪试图表现出友善的样子，
伸出了他的爪子想和小狗握握手：
"哈啰！你好！"

但他却露出了爪子尖利的部分，
小狗就惊慌地逃跑了。

Opening the door, Su asked,
"Teddy, why are you here?"

He blushed, **"My family is moving,
so I came to say goodbye."**

Su giggled, "Oh silly, you didn't have to."
But a loud noise interrupted them.

苏打开了门，她问："泰迪，你为什么在这里？"

他红着脸说："我要搬家了，所以我是来跟你说再见的。"

苏笑着回答："傻瓜，你不必这样做。"
但这时，突然传来一阵声响打断了他们的对话。

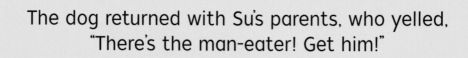

The dog returned with Su's parents, who yelled,
"There's the man-eater! Get him!"

The villagers gave chase, and Teddy fled again.
But unexpectedly, Su followed her new friend into the wild.

小狗和苏的父母一起回来了，大声地喊叫：
"那个会吃人的东西在这里！抓住他！"

村民们追了上来，而泰迪又再一次地逃跑了。
但泰迪没有想到的是，
苏跟着她的新朋友跑到了野外。

In the bush, the pair dashed ahead, and gradually squawks of birds replaced the roar of the crowd.

Su had never ventured beyond her farm before. With Teddy as her guide, she marveled at wondrous sights.

在灌木丛里，他们两个拼命地往前冲，然后慢慢地，树林里的鸟叫声正取代了后面追赶的吼叫声。

苏从来没有跨过农场到更远的地方冒险过。泰迪当苏的向导，而苏对这四周奇妙的景色感到惊奇。

Miles away,
the Queen wondered,
"Where's Teddy?"

The King got wind that humans
had entered the jungle.

Immediately they dropped
everything, and raced
to find their son.

在远处，虎后正想着："泰迪到哪里去了？"
虎王听到风声，知道有人类进入了丛林。

他们立刻放下手边的事，冲去寻找他们的儿子。

On one end of the forest Ma-Ma and Ba-Ba tracked Su's footsteps.
On the other, the King and Queen caught Teddy's scent. Unaware of
the two hunting parties, the girl and tiger innocently hiked along.

妈妈和爸爸在森林的一头寻着苏的足迹往前走。而在森林的另一头，虎王和虎后嗅到了
泰迪的气味。小女孩和小老虎一点儿都没有察觉有人在追踪他们，毫无警觉地往前走去。

The youngsters wandered toward a cliff, where Teddy showed Su the spectacular waterfalls.

As she admired the lovely view, he saw his bright stripes, sharp teeth, and claws in a reflecting pool.

两个小朋友往山崖的方向走去，
泰迪带苏去看壮观的瀑布。

苏欣赏着这些美妙的景色，
泰迪从水池中看到了自己的倒影，
看着自己黄亮亮的斑纹、
尖利的牙齿和爪子。

Teddy always considered
himself like everyone else.
Now why did people dislike
him for being different?
Su didn't mind at all.

While he was lost in thought,
Su accidentally stepped on
a snake, sleeping in the grass!

泰迪总是觉得他和其他人没有什么不一样。
他觉得纳闷，为什么别人会因为他的不同
而不喜欢他呢？但是苏却一点也不介意。

当他想着发呆的时候，苏不小心踩到了
一条正在草丛中睡觉的蛇。

The serpent gave a loud "Hiss!"

Su slipped on a stone. Tipping backwards
over the ledge, she cried, "Help!"

Shaken from his daydream,
Teddy turned in disbelief.
What could he do?

蛇发出"嘶嘶"的声音！

苏一脚踩上了一颗滑溜溜的石头，
脚底一滑，接着又被崖边的岩石绊倒，
身体失去重心而往后仰。苏大声叫："救命啊！"

泰迪从他的白日梦中惊醒，他有些迟疑，
不知道自己能不能帮上忙？

Instinctively the cat leapt forward to save Su.
Bounding into the chasm below,
Teddy shouted,

"Roar!"

小老虎出于本能地跳向前去救苏。
一跃就跃下了深谷，
泰迪大叫：
"吼！"

Slowly opening her eyes, Su was surprised that she had stopped falling. Instead, she saw Teddy's toothy grin. His strong bite held onto her, as his claws clutched the dangling branches of a tree.

苏慢慢地睁开她的眼睛，惊讶地发现，自己不但没有继续往下掉，而且看到泰迪正对着她露齿而笑。泰迪用他强壮的牙齿咬住苏的衣服，再用爪子牢牢地抓紧一棵树的树枝。

With a mighty effort, the tiger dragged the girl up. They rested to catch their breath.

Then Su grabbed onto his tail and Teddy led the way, as they carefully climbed up.

小老虎用尽所有的力气将小女孩往上拉，他们先稍作休息来调整自己的呼吸。

然后，苏抓紧了泰迪的尾巴，跟着泰迪的脚步，小心翼翼地一步一步往上爬。

Hearing their children's voices, the worried parents rushed to them.

Arriving at the same time, they saw Teddy pull Su back to safety.
Confused, each group warily kept their distance.

听到了他们的声音之后，苏和泰迪的父母赶紧跑向他们的孩子。

他们同时来到了山崖边，并且看见泰迪把苏安全地带了回来。
两边的父母都对他们看到的景象感到疑惑，小心翼翼地站在离彼此远远的地方。

The cat and girl knew what to do.
They held their parents' hands
and brought them together.

Ma-Ma and Ba-Ba smiled.
The King was puzzled.
"Dear, our little prince is
growing up indeed," laughed
the Queen.

小老虎和小女孩明白他们这个时候应该
要做些什么。他们拉着自己父母的手，
领着他们往对方走去。

妈妈和爸爸微笑着，但这时虎王却感到困惑。
"亲爱的，我们的小王子的确长大了，"虎后笑着说。

Afterwards, each family invited the other over
to play. Traveling between treetop and rooftop, the
adults were amazed how well everybody got along.
"Good manners make good neighbors," they all agreed.

从此以后，这两家人经常邀请对方到彼此的家里来玩。
从这一家玩到下一家，他们都没有想到大家能相处得如此融洽。
大家都同意这句话："有礼貌、互相友好，
就能交到好的邻居朋友。"

Su and Teddy enjoyed swimming and singing.
They shared nature walks and bedtime stories.

And in the jungle, both man and beast would recall
that this was a terrific Year of the Tiger!

苏和泰迪喜欢一起游泳和唱歌。他们还一起散步、
说说自己喜欢的睡前故事给对方听。

在丛林里，人类和野兽都会记得今年是美好的虎年！

虎

Tiger
1926, 1938, 1950, 1962, 1974, 1986, 1998, 2010, 2022, 2034

People born in the Year of the Tiger are bold and proud. These warm souls are courageous and charismatic. But sometimes they reveal different stripes when they are rash and unpredictable. Though they may seem secretive and catty, tigers prove to be the fiercest of friends.

虎年出生的人个性坚毅、大胆且自负。这些热情的人勇敢，并具有独特的个人魅力。他们个性的另外一面是做事草率且让人摸不着头绪。虽然他们有时候看起来像猫一样的充满神秘，但他们会是你最凶猛的朋友。

Learn about cool inventions from Asia!

"Whatever your age, *The Discovery of Ramen* is an experience to whet your appetite with a subject worth savoring."- Sampan

"[*Fireworks & Gunpowder* has] a simple yet brilliantly explained set of facts worked into the story, and some really gorgeous illustrations" –Read it Daddy

"An appealing, informative read for anime and manga enthusiasts that shows young fans that their favorite comic and animation style has a long and rich history." - *School Library Journal*